P9-CIV-495

Heidi Heckelbeck

Is the Bestest Babysitter!

By Wanda Coven
Illustrated by Priscilla Burris

LITTLE SIMON

New York London Toronto Sydney New Delhi

LITTLE SIMON
An imprint of Simon & Schuster Children's Publishing Division
1230 Avenue of the Americas, New York, New York 10020
First Little Simon hardcover edition December 2015
Copyright © 2015 by Simon & Schuster, Inc.
Also available in a Little Simon paperback edition.
All rights reserved, including the right of reproduction in whole or
in part in any form. LITTLE SIMON is a registered trademark of
Simon & Schuster, Inc., and associated colophon is a trademark of
Simon & Schuster, Inc. For information about special discounts for bulk
purchases, please contact Simon & Schuster Special Sales at 1-866-506-1949
or business@simonandschuster.com. The Simon & Schuster Speakers Bureau
can bring authors to your live event. For more information or to book an event
contact the Simon & Schuster Speakers Bureau at 1-866-248-3049 or visit our
website at www.simonspeakers.com.
Designed by Ciara Gay
Manufactured in the United States of America 1115 FFG
10 9 8 7 6 5 4 3 2 1
Library of Congress Cataloging-in-Publication Data
Coven, Wanda.
Heidi Heckelbeck is the bestest babysitter! / by Wanda Coven ; illustrated by
Priscilla Burris. — First Little Simon paperback edition.
pages cm. — (Heidi Heckelbeck ; 16)
Summary: Heidi teams up with her friends to create a babysitting station at the
Brewster Elementary fair, but when things do not go as smoothly as planned,
Heidi turns to her Book of Spells to find the perfect magical solution.
ISBN 978-1-4814-4631-0 (hc) — ISBN 978-1-4814-4630-3 (pbk) —
ISBN 978-1-4814-4632-7 (eBook)
[1. Witches—Fiction. 2. Babysitters—Fiction. 3. Magic—Fiction.]
I. Burris, Priscilla, illustrator. II. Title.
PZ7.C83393Hk 2015
[Fic]—dc23
2015015520

CONTENTS

Chapter 1

WIGS AND BEARDS

Heidi had her very own classroom in the playroom. She had a chalkboard, a desk, and a pointer. She even had students: a stuffed panda; a stuffed kangaroo; and her little brother, Henry. They all sat on small wooden chairs in front of Heidi, who was, of

course, the teacher. She called herself Mrs. Applegarth.

Mrs. Applegarth tapped the chalkboard with her pointer. "Class, what can you tell me

2

animals do when they're scared?"

Henry raised his hand. Mrs. Applegarth called on him.

"Skunks spray stink bombs when they're scared," he answered. "And octopuses squirt black ink."

"Good answer, Henry," said Mrs. Applegarth. "You get a gold star!"

Heidi handed Henry a gold star sticker.

"Excuse me, Mrs. Applegarth!" said someone from the door.

Heidi pulled off her pretend glasses and looked at the door. It was Mom.

"May I help you, Mrs. Heckelbeck?"

Mom entered the classroom. She had a fancy card in her hand with gold cursive writing on it. Heidi noticed it right away.

"Ooh, what's that?" she asked, forgetting her role as make-believe teacher.

"It's a wedding invitation," Mom said.

"Do we get to go?" Heidi asked.

"It's for grown-ups this time," Mom said. "We'll need to get a babysitter."

"A BABYSITTER?" questioned Heidi. "But why? It's not like I'm a baby anymore."

"That's true," agreed Mom.

"Then what if *I* babysit Henry?" suggested Heidi.

"No way, José!" Henry cried. "I'm

not a baby anymore EITHER!"

"Well, you're more of a baby than I am!" Heidi argued.

"Am not!" Henry said, folding his arms.

"Okay, that's enough," said Mom firmly. "Neither of you are babies, but you're *both* too young to stay home alone."

Heidi ran across the room to the dress-up trunk and put on a gray-haired wig. She stuffed her hair inside like a bathing cap.

"Am I old enough now?" asked Heidi.

Mom shook her head.

"What about me?" Henry asked. He had put on a top hat and beard. "I'm Abraham Lincoln, and he's REALLY old!"

Heidi rolled her eyes at her brother.
"He's not even alive anymore."

"Well, he used to be old," said Henry.

Mom laughed. "Nice try, you two," she said.

Heidi sighed. "But I REALLY want to babysit," she said sadly.

"You'll get to babysit soon enough," Mom said. "But you have to be a little older before I'm comfortable leaving you alone with your brother."

Heidi pulled off the gray wig.

"Well, I won't need THIS," she said, tossing the wig in the trunk. "Because by THEN I'll already be a grandmother!"

Chapter 2

A SPECiAL ANNOUNCEMENT

Heidi tapped her best friend, Lucy Lancaster, on the shoulder.

"Have you ever babysat before?" asked Heidi.

Lucy looked up from her desk. "Nope," she said. "And I wouldn't want to, either."

This surprised Heidi. "Why wouldn't you want to babysit?"

"Because little kids NEVER listen," said Lucy. "And they always get into your stuff."

Heidi raised her eyebrows. "Well, I like to be in charge," she said.

Then their teacher Mrs. Welli stood up and did the "Holy macaroni" routine to get the class's attention.

"Holy!" called out Mrs. Welli.

"Macaroni!" responded the class.

Then the classroom grew quiet.

"Today I have a special announce-ment," Mrs. Welli began.

Everyone listened closely.

"Brewster Elementary is going to hold a school fair to raise money for our new music pro-gram. The fair will be hosted by the second and third grades. That means you'll create the booth activities

and collect the tickets. And the booth that collects the *most* tickets will win a pizza-movie party!"

The class began to chatter with excitement. Mrs. Welli put a finger to her lips.

"Now I want everyone to begin thinking of ideas for your booths.

You can have a booth by yourself or you can have one or two partners. You will also need to ask a teacher to oversee your booth."

Heidi's and Lucy's eyes grew wide.

"Do you want to run a booth together?" asked Heidi.

"Maybe," said Lucy. "What do you have in mind?"

Heidi smiled broadly. "How about a babysitting booth?"

Lucy frowned. "Babysitting is not for me, remember?" she said. "Can you think of anything else?"

Heidi bit her lower lip. "Not really," she said. "I kind of want to do something with babysitting."

"Well, you may have to ask somebody else," Lucy said.

"That's okay," said Heidi. "If I win the prize, I'll invite you to the pizza-movie party."

"And if I win the prize, I'll invite you," said Lucy.

"Deal," said Heidi.

Chapter 3

GO, TEAM!

Heidi looked around the room for a partner. She spied Bruce Bickerson drawing a picture at his desk. Heidi hurried over.

"What's that?" she asked.

Bruce pushed his glasses up the bridge of his nose.

"Plans for a mechanical dog," he said proudly. "It's my latest invention."

"Pretty cool," Heidi said. Then she leaned against his desktop. "So, do

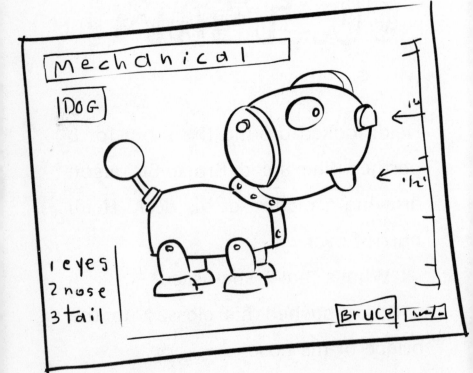

Mechanical
DOG

1 eyes
2 nose
3 tail

Bruce Two-you want to run a babysitting booth with me for the fair?"

Bruce shaded the eye sockets on his dog. "No, thanks," he said. "I'm going to have a science booth."

Heidi scrunched her lips to one side. *Darn,* she thought, but she could hardly be mad. Bruce was the best scientist in the whole school. Of course he would want to run a science booth.

She walked over to Laurel Lambert's desk. "Want to do a babysitting booth with me?" asked Heidi hopefully.

Laurel wrinkled her nose. "I'm already going to have an art studio booth," she said. "You want to do that?"

Heidi loved art, but she had her heart set on babysitting. *I wonder if we could do both?* she thought. Then something clicked in Heidi's head. She ran over and got Bruce. Then she dragged two chairs in front of Laurel's desk.

"What are you up to, Heidi?" asked
Laurel.

"I have an idea," Heidi said, scooch-
ing her chair in. "What if we put all

of our ideas into one booth?"

"What do you mean?" questioned Laurel.

"We could make our own little hands-on museum!" said Heidi.

"Oh, I get it," said Bruce. "We could offer art projects, science projects, and even babysitting for little kids all in one place!"

"Exactly!" said Heidi.

"I like that idea," said Laurel. "But how does babysitting fit in? It's not something you usually see at a museum."

Heidi shrugged it off. "I'm sure I'll think of something fun to go with babysitting," she said. "Are you guys in?"

"I'm in!" said Bruce. "I love activity museums."

"Me too," Laurel said.

Then the three friends named their booth: The Little Explorers' Museum.

Chapter 4

TOP TEACHER

The rest of the class had figured out their special activities by the end of the morning. Now everyone needed to pick a teacher to oversee their booth. Finding the perfect teacher was important, so at lunch Heidi made a list of teachers to choose from.

Mrs. Welli
Mr. Doodlebee
Principal Pennypacker
Mrs. Noddywonks
Mr. Jacobs

She dipped a chicken tender in barbecue sauce and studied the list.

"How about Mrs. Welli?" she asked her teammates.

"I love Mrs. Welli, but she's not the greatest artist,"

Laurel said. "She can only draw stick figures."

Heidi crossed Mrs. Welli off the list.

"How about Mr. Doodlebug?" Heidi always called the art teacher Mr. Doodlebug—even though his name was Mr. Doodlebee.

Laurel gave a thumbs-up. "He'd be perfect for the

art studio. Plus he could help decorate our museum."

"I object," said Bruce. "He's not science-y enough for me."

"Okay, scratch Mr. Doodlebug," said Heidi, crossing his name off the list. "What about Principal Pennypacker?"

"He'll probably be too busy," said Laurel. "I mean the whole school is coming, including parents. I'm sure they will all want to talk to him."

"Hmm. Mrs. Noddywonks?" Heidi continued down her list.

Mrs. Noddywonks was the drama teacher.

"She's definitely artistic," said Laurel. "Have you seen the sets she makes for the plays?"

"Love them," said Heidi. "Especially that fairy castle set she made for *Beauty and the Beast.*"

"She's into science, too," Bruce added. "One time she volunteered to be the pilot in my floating lawn chair experiment."

Laurel's eyes widened. "Your what?" she asked.

"I tried to send a lawn chair across Lake Carolina with balloons and a fan," said Bruce proudly. "I couldn't even get Mrs. Noddywonks in the water!"

Heidi shot Bruce, a look. "Because
the lawn chair folded up on poor
Mrs. Noddywonks!" she said.

"She was really nice about it," said Bruce. "She said she had never been eaten by a lawn chair before."

The girls burst into laughter.

"Okay," said Heidi, still laughing. "Nod if you want Mrs. Noddywonks."

Bruce and Laurel nodded like crazy.

"Mrs. Noddywonks WINS!" declared Heidi.

Chapter 5

THE WINNING IDEA

Everybody talked about the school fair at recess.

"Natalie and I are going to have a dunk tank," said Lucy.

"Well, that'll make a big SPLASH!" Heidi said, poking Lucy in the ribs. "Get it? Splash?"

Lucy rolled her eyes and laughed.

"Who are you going to dunk?" asked Charlie Chen.

"I'm not sure yet," Lucy said. "But it has to be someone important that kids will want to see soaked!"

They all tried to imagine who that someone would be.

"So, what are you doing for the fair, Charlie?" asked Heidi.

"Not getting dunked!" he said, laughing. "I'm going to run a lemonade stand. I have a secret recipe for fresh-squeezed lemonade with the juice of twenty-five lemons."

Heidi sucked in her cheeks and made a sour lemon face.

"Don't worry, silly," said Charlie. "I'll sweeten it!"

"My booth will have something sweet too!" said Eve Etsy excitedly. "I'm going to have a bakery booth with confetti cupcakes and home-made s'mores bars!"

Natalie Newman licked her lips. "I'm definitely going to visit YOUR booth!"

"Me too!" said Lucy and Heidi at the same time.

Then Heidi tapped Stanley Stonewrecker on the shoulder. "And what are you doing?" she asked.

"I'm going to set up a miniature golf course," said Stanley.

"Wow, that's such a cool idea!" said Heidi.

"Not as cool as MY idea!" inter-rupted Melanie Maplethorpe, who had barged her way into the middle of the group.

Lucy rolled her eyes at Melanie. "So, what's YOUR big idea?" she asked.

Melanie stuck her nose in the air. "It just so happens that I'M NOT TELLING," she said.

Then she waved Stanley over. He rushed to Melanie's side. She whispered into his ear. Stanley nodded.

"And DON'T TELL!" Melanie said loudly. Then she turned to the rest of the group.

"Well, it looks like Stanley changed his mind," she said. "Now he's on MY team because Stanley knows *I* have the winning idea." Then she walked off, and Stanley followed close behind.

Heidi kicked a pebble on the playground.

"Merg. We don't stand a chance of winning the pizza-movie party now," she complained.

Laurel folded her arms. "Says WHO?" she declared. "Just because Melanie has a BIG MOUTH doesn't mean she's going to win!"

"That's right!" agreed Bruce. "Melanie's just trying to scare us."

Heidi looked at her friends thankfully. "You guys are right," she said. "I'm not going to let Smell-a-nie spoil my fun either!"

Chapter 6

WHO WOULD DO THAT?

The Little Explorers stopped by the auditorium after school. They told Mrs. Noddywonks about the museum idea and asked her to oversee their booth.

"I'd love to!" said Mrs. Noddywonks. "What a clever idea!"

Then Mrs. Noddywonks suggested the museum be set up in a classroom next to the gymnasium.

"That way you'll have more room," she said. "And we can make signs that point to the museum."

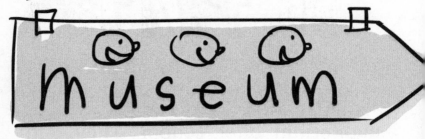

The Little Explorers thanked Mrs. Noddywonks. Then they caught the school bus to Heidi's house.

Mrs. Heckelbeck welcomed Heidi and her friends. She made pinwheel sandwiches and apple slices for everyone. Laurel called the meeting to order.

"Okay, let's go over what every-one's doing," said Laurel.

"You first," Heidi said.

Laurel brushed a wisp of blond hair out of her eyes.

"Okay, for my art studio, I'll bring in a bunch of art stuff, like crayons, markers, sequins, glitter glue, paints,

paper, brushes, and stickers. I'll also need some tables and chairs and a place to hang the finished art."

"That sounds great," said Heidi. "Mrs. Noddywonks can help with the tables and chairs."

Laurel nodded. "What about you, Bruce?" she asked. "What do you have planned for your activity?"

"I plan to set up my latest inven-

tions," said Bruce. "Then I'll show the kids how they work and let them try each one."

"Wow! Which inventions are you going to bring?" Heidi asked.

"I'll bring the Bicker Picker-Upper and the Bicker Sticker," said Bruce. "I'm also going to bring my latest invention, the Bicker Barker."

"Is that the robot dog you were drawing at school?" asked Heidi.

"Yup. You wanna see?"

The girls nodded eagerly.

57

Bruce pulled his drawing from his backpack and laid it on the table.

"I used my dog, Frankie, as a model," he said.

"Will it really work?" asked Laurel.

"I hope so!" said Bruce. "It should be able to walk, bark, and pick things up in its mouth."

"Will the robot dog bite, too?" Laurel asked, pointing to its mouth.

Bruce smiled craftily. "Only if I tell it to," he said. The girls laughed.

"Okay, your turn, Heckelbeck," said Laurel. "What do you have planned for the booth?"

Heidi looked at her friends and blinked. She had no idea what to do. "Uh, so far just babysitting," she admitted.

"But what are you going to DO when you babysit?" asked Bruce.

"That's easy," said Heidi. "I'll watch the little kids."

Bruce looked confused. "But who would buy a ticket for that?"

"He's right," said Laurel. "No one would go to a boring babysitter booth. You need some kind of activity to make it fun for the kids."

Heidi sat back down and leaned on her elbows. She knew they were right. She had only wanted to babysit so she could prove she was good at it.

"Okay, okay, I'll come up with a better plan," she said. "Can I let you know tomorrow?"

Laurel and Bruce looked at each other.

"Okay," said Laurel. "But make sure it's something fun."

"It will be," said Heidi. "I promise."

Chapter 7

CONFETTI AND STREAMERS

"What's the matter, pumpkin?" asked Mom.

Heidi slumped onto the sofa. Her friends had gone home and left Heidi with a big problem.

"I need an activity for our Little Explorers' Museum," she said. "And

I can't think of anything good."

Mom smiled. "Well, just pick something *you* like to do," she suggested.

"Oh but what?" mumbled Heidi.

"How about tap-dancing?" Mom suggested.

"But I'm not good enough to teach anyone," said Heidi.

"Then what about dress-up?" Mom said. "You could

bring your dress-up trunk to school and take pictures of kids in costume."

"But then my dress-up clothes would get wrecked," said Heidi.

Mom rested her hand on Heidi's shoulder.

"I'm sure you'll think of some-thing," she said. "Just ask yourself, 'What do I really *love* to do?'"

So Heidi thought really hard. She liked to bake cookies, but there wasn't an oven in the classroom. She liked to knit and read, but those were probably too quiet to win a bunch of tickets. *Is there anything I love to do that's SPECTACULAR?* she asked her-self. Then a sly grin spread over her face.

Magic! she thought. *I can perform a dazzling magic trick!*

Heidi loved to use her witching skills. She hopped off of the sofa and raced to her bedroom. Then she reached under her bed and pulled out her trusty *Book of Spells* and Witches of Westwick medallion.

She thumbed through the pages and found a chapter called Marvelous Magic Tricks. Then she put her finger on a trick called Rainbow Confetti Fountain. She read over the spell.

Rainbow Confetti Fountain

Have you ever wanted to perform magic tricks for your friends and fellow witches? Perhaps you're the kind of witch who loves to entertain children. If you like to be festive and show off your witching skills, then this is the spell for you!

Ingredients:

4 sheets of colored paper cut into long strips

A pinch of red chili pepper flakes

A dollop of whipped cream

1 package of blue raspberry Cracklers

Combine the ingredients in a top hat. Hold your Witches of Westwick medallion in one hand and place your other hand over the hat. Chant the following spell:

CALLING ALL FRIENDS!

CALLING ALL DREAMERS!

BRING FORTH A FOUNTAIN OF

CONFETTI AND STREAMERS!

Important note: As soon as you've chanted the spell, remove your hand from the hat.

Heidi ran through the list of ingredients. "I'm pretty sure we have all this stuff," she said to herself. She knew her dad had some Cracklers candy in his lab. He had used them in his Sizzling Soda recipe.

Heidi got right to work. She opened her desk drawer and pulled out four sheets of colored paper: red, yellow, blue, and white.

Then she hurried downstairs.

Nobody was around. She quickly placed a pinch of red chili pepper flakes into a snack bag and zipped it. Then she grabbed a tub of whipped cream from the fridge and put all the ingredients into a shopping bag, along with a spoon.

Next she snuck into the lab and borrowed a package of blue raspberry Cracklers from her dad's secret-ingredients drawer.

Well, she said to herself triumphantly, *we might just win this pizza-movie party after all!* Then she smuggled everything up to her room.

Chapter 8

TiCKET TROUBLE

"I'm SO excited!" Heidi said on the night of the fair. She skipped across the Brewster Elementary playground. She had on Henry's silver silk cape, a top hat, and her Witches of Westwick medallion around her neck.

"Me too!" agreed Laurel, skipping

along beside her. "It's so fun to come to school AT NIGHT."

"It's kind of weirdly magical," said Bruce.

Heidi hopped through the hopscotch squares.

"I LOVE magic!" said Heidi. She couldn't wait to perform her special trick.

Heidi, Laurel, and Bruce set up their activity stations in the classroom next to the gym. Mrs. Noddywonks helped them arrange tables and chairs. She had made a sign for each station: There was BICKER'S BEAKERS for the science lab, THE HANDPRINT ART STUDIO for Laurel's station, and THE MAGIC HATTERY for Heidi's station. She had also helped the children make a sign that said THE LITTLE EXPLORERS' MUSEUM. Each station had a

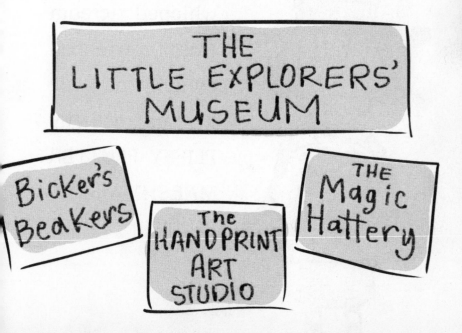

table and balloons. Bruce and Laurel's stations both had tents. Heidi had a small platform stage that faced the circle-time rug.

Heidi laid a red velvet cloth across her table. She set her magic ingredi-ents on top—then she noticed her whipped cream wasn't whipped cream at all! It was actually FLIFFY FLUTTER MARSHMALLOW BUTTER! She

looked at the clock. *Well, it's too late now. Let's hope it works!*

When the museum was all set up, the Little Explorers went to the gym to see the other booths. First they stopped by Lucy and Natalie's dunk tank.

"So, who is crazy enough to get dunked?" asked Bruce.

Lucy smiled and looked at someone behind them.

"I AM!" said a man.

The kids whirled around.

"Principal Pennypacker!" Bruce squealed.

Both Laurel and Heidi squealed, too!

The principal was dressed like a clown.

"You kids look surprised!" he said.

"We ARE!" said the children.

Principal Pennypacker laughed. "Well, I'm doing it for my favorite cause—our school!"

"Wow, Lucy, I'll bet your booth wins the prize with HIM in the tank!" said Heidi.

Lucy pumped her fist. "Let's hope so!" she said.

Then the Little Explorers visited the other booths.

"Look!" shouted Heidi, pointing her finger. "Melanie and Stanley are running the ticket booth!"

Melanie looked up when she heard her name. She had a stack of tickets

in her hand. She waved them at Heidi as if it were a stack of hundred-dollar bills.

"That's right, and I have ALL the tickets," she said proudly. "Which means WE'RE going to win the pizza-movie party!"

Heidi looked at Bruce and Laurel and then back at Melanie.

"But don't you know the ticket booth *gives* the tickets to the customers?" asked Heidi.

"Heidi's right," said Laurel. "You'll be collecting money—not tickets!"

Melanie looked at the stack of tickets in her hand. It hadn't occurred to her that she'd have to give them all away.

"But we'll get the tickets back at the end—isn't that right, Stanley?"

Stanley shrugged. He had just gone along with what Melanie had told him.

"I think Heidi and Laurel might be right," he said uncomfortably.

Melanie smacked herself in the forehead with the palm of her hand. "Why didn't you TELL ME?!" she cried.

Melanie threw the tickets down, and tears welled in her eyes.

Heidi spoke up. "For what it's worth, Melanie, I think handing out tickets makes you one of the most important booths. Thank you for helping everyone out."

Sniffling, Melanie took a deep breath, dried her eyes, and calmed down. "Thanks, Heidi," she said in a low voice.

Heidi smiled and turned to Bruce and Laurel. "Okay, Little Explorers, let's go have some fun!"

Chapter 9

A NEW TWIST

A long line of parents with younger children formed outside the Little Explorers' Museum. Heidi stood at the door and collected tickets in an empty coffee can. Then Mrs. Noddywonks led the children to the craft table and science lab. She had to set up extra

tables and chairs to handle the crowd.

Laurel got the kids right to work.
They pressed their palms into pie
tins filled with paint.
Then they made
handprints on their

papers. Laurel showed them how to make handprint flamingos and kissing fish. Then she hung the finished artwork with clothespins on a line made from kitchen string.

Using a remote control, Bruce picked up all kinds of toys with the Bicker Picker-Upper. The children shrieked with laughter when he picked up a pair of underwear. Then Bruce rolled a ball across the floor.

"Fetch!" he commanded.

With a push of another button on his remote control, the Bicker Barker bounded after the ball.

"Again! Again!" the kids shouted. Bruce had his robot dog bring the ball to each child so everyone could play robo-fetch.

Then it was Heidi's turn. The children sat down on the rug in front of the stage. Bruce and Laurel joined them. Heidi hopped onto her stage and slipped on a pair of white gloves. Mrs. Noddywonks stood beside the stage with an electric piano. She pushed a button and a short drum-roll played.

Heidi looked at her audience and raised her arms.

"Ladies and gentlemen, boys and girls of all ages! I, the Great Heidini, shall now perform the most spectacular, mega-magical, super-special,

amazing trick!" she said dramatically.

Mrs. Noddywonks pushed another button, and the sound of horns played *Ta-da!*

Heidi pulled off her hat and set it on the table.

"And for this trick, we will need to use several magnificently magical ingredients!"

Mrs. Noddywonks pressed the *Ta-da!* button again.

"First I'll place these special strips of colored paper into my hat!" Heidi held the shreds of paper up. They looked like a rainbow pom-pom!

Then she plopped the paper inside.

Mrs. Noddywonks pressed another button that went *Cha-ching!*

"And now I shall add a pinch of . . ." Heidi paused. She didn't want to reveal the actual ingredients for the spell. With a smile and in her best dramatic voice, Heidi continued, "Red-hot dragon scales!"

Cha-ching! went the keyboard. The kids in the audience murmured and leaned in closer. They were excited to see what Heidi would do next.

"We need a dollop of fairy dreams!" Heidi crossed her fingers and placed the Fliffy Flutter in the hat.

Cha-ching!

"And last but not least, bright blue

mermaid pearls!" She dropped in the
Cracklers and they sizzled.

Cha-ching!

"And now I, the Great Heidini, will
chant the mystical magic words!"
said Heidi.

Mrs. Noddywonks pressed the
drumroll button.

Then Heidi placed one hand over

the hat and the other hand on her medallion. She looked up at the ceiling and shut her eyes. *Oh, please let this work!* she said to herself.

Then Heidi chanted the spell: "Calling all friends! Calling all dreamers! Bring forth a fountain of confetti and streamers!"

The hat began to quiver and quake. She quickly

removed her hand and stood back.
POOF! A fountain of streamers and
confetti rained down on the audience.

"Ooooh!" exclaimed the children.
"Aahhhhh!"

A strip of glittering paper landed
in front of each child.

The children picked up the sparkly pieces of paper. Each one had something written on it.

"Mine says 'Grow your own dinosaur!'" said a boy with spiky brown hair. "I LOVE dinosaurs!"

"Mine says 'Fly like a super-hero!'" said a girl with blond curls. "Wow, I've always wanted to FLY!"

"I have one that says 'Sing like a superstar!'" said a girl with pigtails. "What should we do with them?"

Wow, thought Heidi as she jumped down from the stage. *The spell worked, but the Fliffy Flutter Marshmallow Butter gave it a new twist.* Heidi decided to turn it into an activity for the kids.

"Well, this is a build-your-own-magic-spell workshop!" Heidi said.

"How does it work?" asked Mrs. Noddywonks.

"Everyone should make up a magic spell to go with your slip of paper," said Heidi. "Make up the ingredients and invent a magic rhyme."

"How clever!" exclaimed Mrs. Noddywonks.

Everyone clapped and cheered for Heidi. Then the children began to make up their spells. Laurel and Bruce ran up to Heidi.

"Heidi, HOW in the world did you DO THAT?" asked Laurel.

"Yeah," said Bruce. "That was like REAL magic!"

Heidi smiled craftily. "A true magician must never reveal her secrets!"

Chapter 10

THE MOST TICKETS

"Congratulations to the students of Brewster Elementary!" said Principal Pennypacker. "I'm happy to say we've raised enough money for our new music program!"

The children clapped and whistled.

"And now it's time to announce a

winner for the booth that collected the MOST tickets. As you all know, the winner will get a special pizza-movie party!"

Then they watched Mrs. Crosby hand Principal Pennypacker an envelope.

Lucy grabbed Heidi's arm. "I hope it's YOU!" she whispered.

"No, I hope it's YOU!" Heidi excit-edly whispered back.

They squeezed each other's arms as Principal Pennypacker announced the winner.

"It was a very close race, but the prize goes to . . . the Little Explorers' Museum!"

"I KNEW IT!" said Lucy as everyone hooted and clapped again.

"Will the winners please stand up?" asked the principal.

The Little Explorers' team members jumped up and hugged one another. All the children cheered even louder.

The next Friday night, Heidi, Laurel, and Bruce invited the families who had visited the Little Explorers' Museum to an extra-special-thank-you pizza-movie party at the school. Henry and Lucy came too.

And as it turned out, the party fell on the same night that Heidi's parents were going out to the wedding. She and Henry didn't need a babysitter after all! But Heidi had fun watching over the kids at the party.

"Wow," said Henry with a mouthful of pizza. "You sure are the bestest babysitter."

"You're the bestest magician, too!" added Laurel. "What's your secret?"

Heidi blushed.

"Oh, it's nothing," she said. "I just always like to keep a few good tricks up my sleeve—that's all."

Check out the next book starring **HEIDI HECKELBECK**

"Ho hum." Heidi sighed as she doodled a daisy on her science folder.

Heidi was having a ho-hum morning. She had on a ho-hum outfit. All her favorite clothes were in the wash. She had eaten a bowl of ho-hum oatmeal for breakfast. Henry got the last waffle. And now Heidi and her whole class had to sit and

An excerpt from *Heidi Heckelbeck Makes a Wish*

wait for their teacher Mrs. Welli.

Soon the classroom door squeaked open. Principal Pennypacker followed Mrs. Welli to the front of the room.

Mrs. Welli smiled and clasped her hands. "Principal Pennypacker has a special announcement to make," she said. Then she stepped to one side.

The principal patted the tufts of hair on either side of his head and said, "Good morning, class. I have exciting news. Next week the second grade will go on a field trip to the botanical gardens."

The class cheered.

An excerpt from *Heidi Heckelbeck Makes a Wish*

"You'll take the school bus to get to the gardens," he explained. "Then you'll see flowers, you'll see trees shaped like animals, and you'll even get to play hide-and-seek in a hedge maze. At the end of the morning you'll have a class picnic in a fairy garden, followed by ice-cream bars."

"Yay!" sang the class as they bounced up and down in their seats.

And just like that, Heidi's morning had changed from ho-hum to a real humdinger!

An excerpt from *Heidi Heckelbeck Makes a Wish*